There's a Bison BOUNCING on the Bed!

by Paul Bright

Illustrated by Chris Chatterton

BOUNCING BASICS

tiger tales

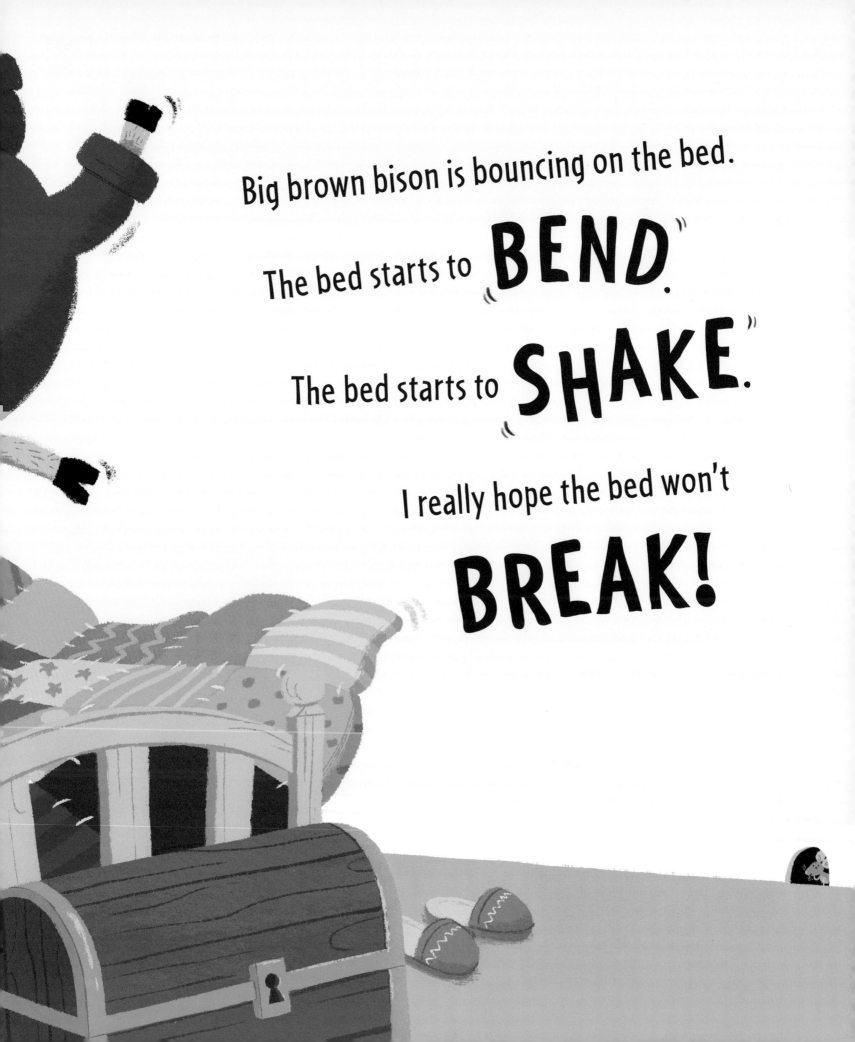

Big brown bison is bouncing on the bed.

The bed starts to "BEND."

The bed starts to "SHAKE."

I really hope the bed won't

BREAK!

Aardvark says,
"That looks like fun.
I think there's room
for more than one!"

Chipmunk says,
"I'll jump with you.
I'm sure there's room
for more than two!"

Then Beetle says,
"Make way for me!
There must be room
for more than three!"

Oh, what a
"thump"
and
"bump"
they make.
I really hope
the bed
won't ...

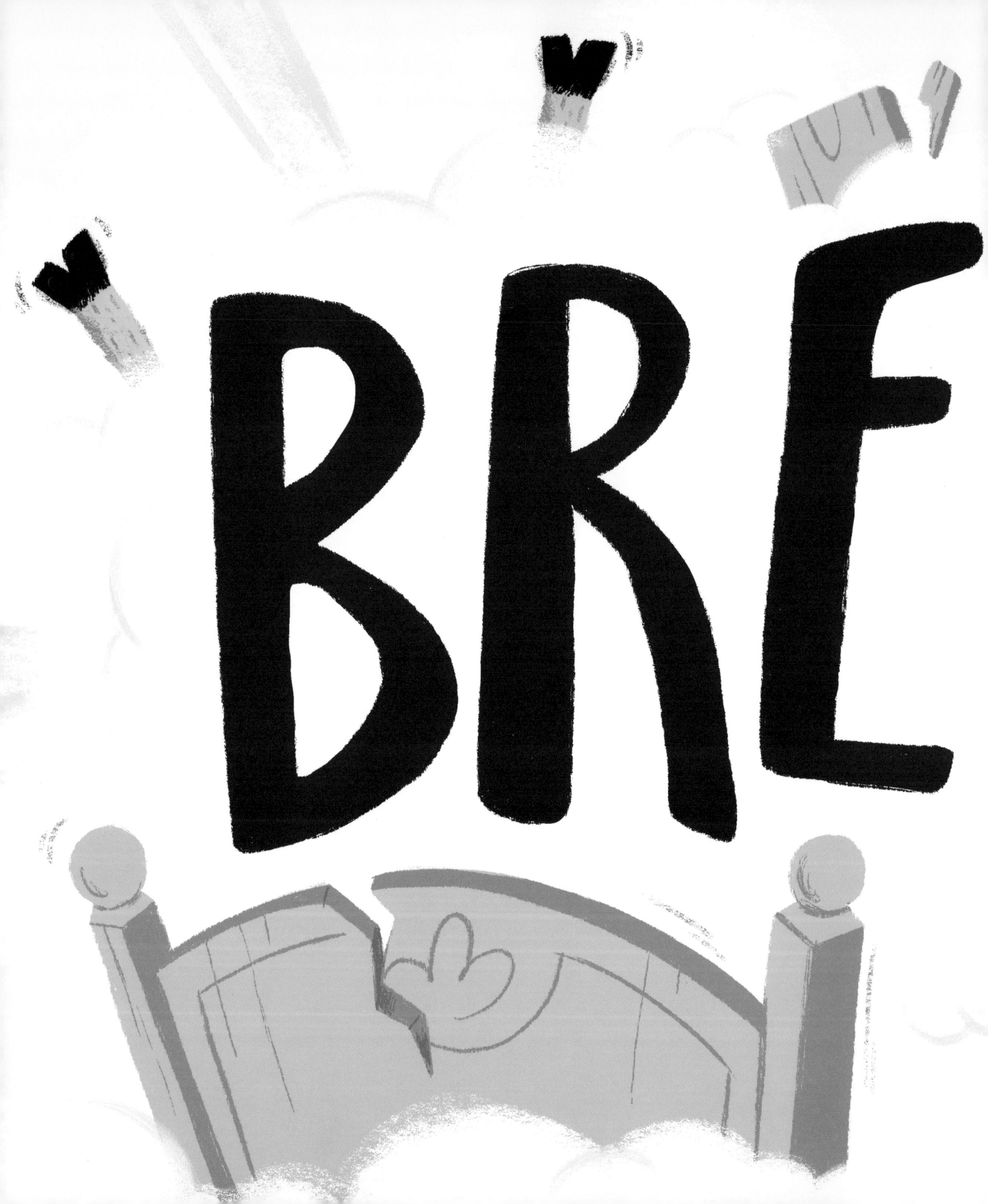
BRE

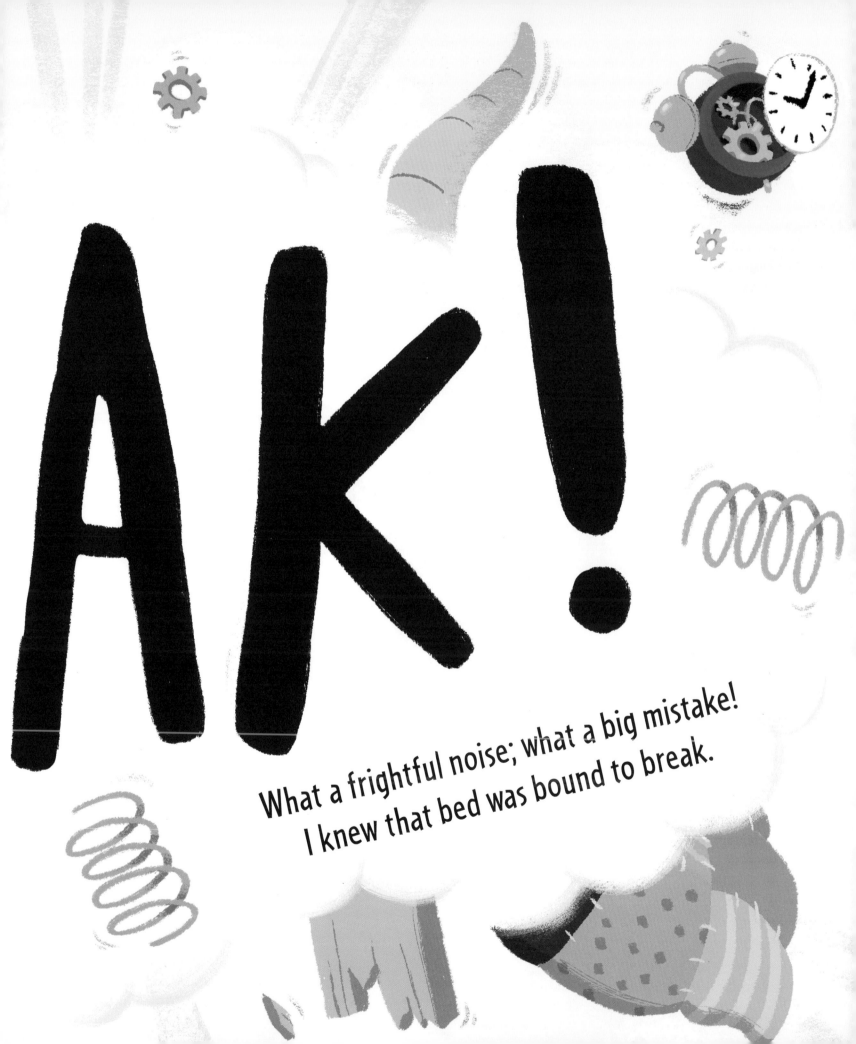

AK!

What a frightful noise; what a big mistake!
I knew that bed was bound to break.

Bison says,
"Look what you've done!
It was all right with only one!"

Aardvark says,
"It must be you!
It didn't break when there were two."

Chipmunk says,
"It wasn't me!
The bed was strong enough for three."

"Stop!"

shouts beetle.

"It's still shaking!
Yes, it is—the bed's still quaking!
Can't you see—there's no mistaking—
Something in the bed is waking!"

Grizzly Bear—for that's his name—
Wakes up and says,

"You're all to blame!
You've all been bouncing on my bed,
And on my tummy and my head!

"Now find a hammer,
nails, and glue,
And make my bed
as good as new."

They fix and mend until it's done.

"**NOW,**"

growls Bear,

"it's time for . . ."

FUN!

For I and J, the best bed-bouncers in the world

~ P. B.

For Hilda & Cyril

~ C. C.

tiger tales
5 River Road, Suite 128, Wilton, CT 06897
Published in the United States 2016
Originally published in Great Britain 2016
by Little Tiger Press
Text copyright © 2016 Paul Bright
Illustrations copyright © 2016 Chris Chatterton
ISBN-13: 978-1-68010-006-8
ISBN-10: 1-68010-006-8
Printed in China
LTP/1800/1243/0815

10 9 8 7 6 5 4 3 2 1

For more insight and activities, visit us at www.tigertalesbooks.com

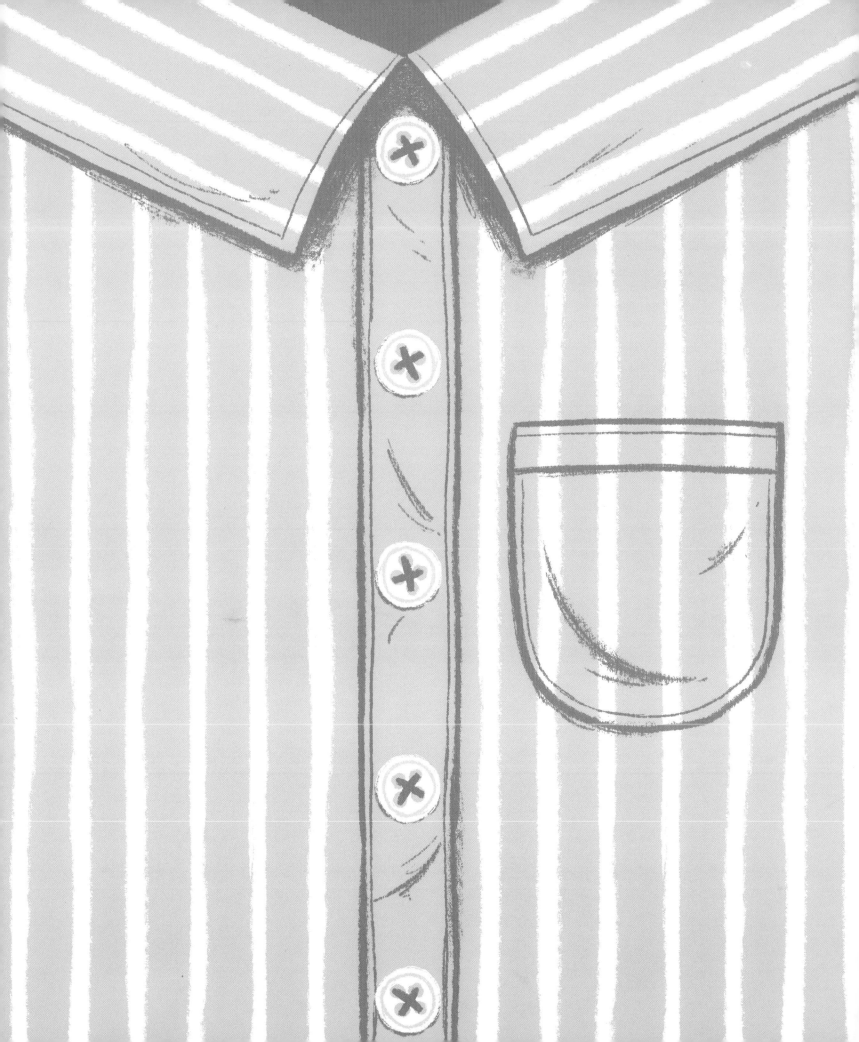